HORRiD HENRY'S
Swimming Lesson

HORRiD HENRY'S
Swimming Lesson

Francesca Simon
Illustrated by Tony Ross

Orion
Children's Books

Horrid Henry's Swimming Lesson first appeared in
Horrid Henry and the Mummy's Curse
first published in Great Britain in 2000 by Orion Children's Books
This edition first published in Great Britain in 2017
by Hodder and Stoughton

3 5 7 9 10 8 6 4

Text © Francesca Simon, 2000
Illustrations © Tony Ross, 2000, 2017

A CIP catalogue record for this book
is available from the British Library.

ISBN 978 1 5101 0198 2

Printed and bound in China

The paper and board used in this book are from well-managed forests
and other responsible sources.

Orion Children's Books
An imprint of
Hachette Children's Group
Part of Hodder & Stoughton
Carmelite House
50 Victoria Embankment
London EC4Y 0DZ

An Hachette UK Company
www.hachette.co.uk
www.orionchildrensbooks.co.uk
www.horridhenry.co.uk

There are many more
Horrid Henry Early Reader books available.

For a complete list visit:
www.orionchildrensbooks.co.uk
or
www.horridhenry.co.uk

Contents

Chapter 1

Oh no! thought Horrid Henry.
He pulled the duvet tightly over his
head. It was Thursday. Horrible,
horrible Thursday. The worst day
of the week.

Horrid Henry was certain Thursdays came more often than any other day. Thursday was his class swimming day.

MONDAY	TUESDAY	WEDNESDAY	THURSDAY	FRIDAY	SATURDAY	SUNDAY
	1	2	3	4	5	6
7	8	9	10	11	12	13
14	15	16	17	18	19	20
21	22	23	24	25	26	27
28	29					

FEBRUARY

Henry had a nagging feeling that this Thursday was even worse than all the other awful Thursdays.

Arrrgh!

Now he remembered. Today was test day. The terrible day when everyone had to show how far they could swim.

Aerobic Al was going for gold.

Moody Margaret was going for silver.

The only ones who were still trying for their five-metre badges were Lazy Linda and Horrid Henry.

Five whole metres! How could
anyone swim such a vast distance!

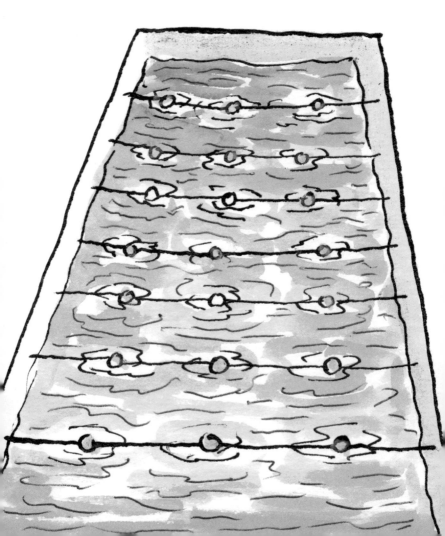

If only they were tested on who
could sink to the bottom of
the pool the fastest,

or splash the most,

or spit water the furthest,

then Horrid Henry would have
every badge in a jiffy.

But no. He had to leap into a freezing cold pool, and, if he survived the shock, somehow thrash his way across five whole metres without drowning.

Well, there was no way he was
going to school today.

Chapter 2

Mum came into his room.
"I can't go to school today, Mum,"
Henry moaned. "I feel terrible."

Mum didn't even look at him.
"Thursday-itis again, I presume?"
said Mum.

"No way!" said Henry. "I didn't even know it was Thursday."

"Get up Henry," said Mum. "You're going swimming and that's that."

Perfect Peter peeked round the door.
"It's badge day today!" he said.
"I'm going for 50 metres!"

"That's brilliant, Peter," said Mum.
"I bet you're the best swimmer in
your class." Perfect Peter
smiled modestly.

"I just try my best," he said.
"Good luck with your five-metre
badge, Henry," he added.

Horrid Henry growled and attacked.
He was a Venus flytrap slowly
mashing a frantic fly between
his deadly leaves.

"Eeeeeowwww!"
screeched Peter.

"Stop being horrid, Henry!"
screamed Mum. "Leave your
poor brother alone!"

Horrid Henry let Peter go.

If only he could find some way not to take his swimming test he'd be the happiest boy in the world.

Chapter 3

Henry's class arrived at the pool.

Right, thought Henry. Time to unpack his excuses to Soggy Sid. "I can't go swimming. I've got a verruca," lied Henry.

"Take off your sock,"
ordered Soggy Sid.
Rats, thought Henry.

"Maybe it's better now," said Henry.
"I thought so," said Sid.

Horrid Henry grabbed his stomach.
"Tummy pains!" he moaned.
"I feel terrible."

"You seemed fine when you
were prancing round the pool a
moment ago," snapped Sid.
"Now get changed."

Time for a killer excuse.
"I forgot my swimming costume!"
said Henry. This was his
best chance of success.

"No problem," said Soggy Sid.
He handed Henry a bag.
"Put on one of these."

Slowly, Horrid Henry rummaged
in the bag. He pulled out
a bikini top,

a blue costume with a hole
in the middle,

a pair of pink pants,

a tiny pair of green trunks,

a polka-dot one piece with bunnies,

see-through white shorts,

and a nappy.

"I can't wear any of these!"
protested Horrid Henry.

"You can and you will, if I have
to put them on you myself,"
snarled Sid.

Horrid Henry squeezed into the
green trunks. He could
barely breathe.

Slowly, he joined the rest of his class
pushing and shoving by the side
of the pool.

Chapter 4

Everyone had millions of badges
sewn all over their costumes.
You couldn't even see Aerobic Al's
bathing suit beneath the stack
of badges.

"Hey you!" shouted Soggy Sid. He pointed at Weepy William. "Where's your swimming costume?"

Weepy William glanced down and burst into tears.
"Waaaaah," he wailed, and ran weeping back to the changing room.

"Now get in!" ordered Soggy Sid.

"But I'll drown!" screamed Henry.
"I can't swim!"
"Get in!" screamed Soggy Sid.

Goodbye, cruel world. Horrid Henry
held his breath and fell into the
icy water.

ARRRRGH!

He was turning into an iceberg!

He was dying! He was dead!
His feet flailed madly as he sank down,

down,

down . . .

. . . clunk!

Henry's feet touched the bottom.
Henry stood up, choking
and spluttering. He was
waist-deep in water.

"Linda and Henry! Swim five
metres – now!"

What am I going to do? thought
Henry. It was so humiliating not
even being able to swim five metres.
Everyone would tease him.
And he'd have to listen to them
bragging about their badges.

Wouldn't it be great to get a badge?
Somehow?

Lazy Linda set off, very very slowly.
Horrid Henry grabbed on to her leg.
Maybe she'll pull me across,
he thought.

"Ugggh!" gurgled Lazy Linda.

"Leave her alone!" shouted Sid.
"Last chance, Henry."

Horrid Henry ran along the pool's bottom and flapped his arms, pretending to swim.

"Did it!" said Henry.

Soggy Sid scowled.
"I said swim, not walk!" screamed
Sid. "You've failed. Now over to
the far lane and practise. Remember,
anyone who stops swimming during
the test doesn't get a badge."

Horrid Henry stomped over to the far lane. No way was he going to practise! How he hated swimming!

Chapter 5

He watched the others splashing up and down, up and down. There was Aerobic Al, doing his laps like a bolt of lightning. And Moody Margaret. And Kung-Fu Kate.

Everyone would be getting a badge
but Henry. It was so unfair.

"Pssst, Susan," said Henry.
"Have you heard? There's a shark
in the deep end!"

"Oh yeah, right," said Sour Susan. She looked at the dark water in the far end of the pool.

"Don't believe me," said Henry. "Find out the hard way. Come back with a leg missing."

Sour Susan paused and whispered something to Moody Margaret.

"Shut up, Henry," said Margaret. They swam off.

"Don't worry about the shark,
Andrew," said Henry.
"I think he's already eaten today."

"What shark?" said Anxious Andrew.
Andrew stared at the deep end. It did
look awfully dark down there.

"Start swimming, Andrew!"
shouted Soggy Sid.

"I don't want to," said Andrew.

"Swim! Or I'll bite you myself!"
snarled Sid.

Andrew started swimming.

"Dave, Ralph, Clare, and Bert — start swimming!" bellowed Soggy Sid.

"Look out for the shark!" said Horrid Henry.

He watched Aerobic Al tearing up
and down the lane. "Gotta swim,
gotta swim, gotta swim," muttered
Al between strokes.

What a show-off, thought Henry.

Wouldn't it be fun to play
a trick on him?

Chapter 6

Horrid Henry pretended he
was a crocodile.

He sneaked under the water to the
middle of the pool and waited until
Aerobic Al swam overhead.

Then Horrid Henry reached up.

Pinch! Henry grabbed Al's thrashing
leg. Tee hee, thought Horrid Henry.

"AAAARGGG!"

screamed Al.

"Something's grabbed my leg.

Help!"

Aerobic Al leaped out of the pool.

"It's a shark!" screamed Sour Susan.
She scrambled out of the pool.

"There's a shark in the pool!"
screeched Anxious Andrew.

"There's a shark in the pool!"
howled Rude Ralph.

Everyone was screaming and
shouting and struggling to get out.

The only one left in the pool was Henry.

Shark!

Horrid Henry forgot there were no
sharks in swimming pools.

Horrid Henry forgot he'd started
the shark rumour.

Horrid Henry forgot he
couldn't swim.

All he knew was that he was
alone in the pool – with a

shark!

Horrid Henry swam for his life.

Shaking and quaking, splashing and crashing, he torpedoed his way to the side of the pool and scrambled out.

He gasped and panted. Thank
goodness. Safe at last! He'd never
ever go swimming again.

"Five metres!" bellowed Soggy Sid. "You've all failed your badges today, except for – Henry!"

"Whoopee!" screamed Henry. "Olympics here I come!"

"Waaaaaaahhhhhh!"

wailed the other children.

What are you going to read next?

Don't miss more mischief with
Horrid Henry . . .

Henry has a very
smelly plan to
defeat Margaret in
**Horrid Henry's
Stinkbomb**,

and plays
the ultimate prank
on Perfect Peter in
**Horrid Henry and
the Mega-Mean
Time Machine**.

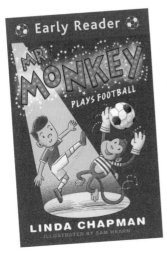

Or for more sporty stories, discover the magic of **Mr Monkey Plays Football**,

and join the Weirdibeasts for fun and games in **Weird Sports Day**.

Visit
www.orionchildrensbooks.co.uk
to discover all the Early Readers